HARE'S JOURNEY

By Sandra Bright

Dedicated with love to my grand-children,

Jasmine and Molly.

࿔

My story begins in the English countryside, in a valley, somewhere not far from a gently flowing river, near a tranquil wood. Where, in a hidden spot, cocooned in soft green moss, amongst twisted roots, tiny leverets quiver and twitch, watch and listen, and sometimes dream...

Asleep amongst the briars lies a Hare,

Dreaming,

Warmed by a shaft of early morning sunshine that slants through the twisted stems.

Shadows dance on a brindled kaleidoscope of grey-russet fur.

Her dreams are remote memories; etched by time, not by familiarity.

Sagas and traditions inscribed in the stones, chiselled in the bark of aged oaks.

Myths washed up in the ripples of a river's surface.

A passing Poet-Wanderer, shrouded in mist, recalls the distant voices of storytellers.

Hare twitches.

The witch scuttles towards her den.

The hunter meets her with a stinging arrow.

Hare dreams of hounds, sleek dun bodies, yellow teeth,

dripping white spittle.

Eyes blazing, slits of red.

An old woman sits rocking, nursing a bleeding hand.

A young shoot braves the chilly haze, its unexpected

dewiness gives a shock of pleasure. The Poet observes,

records, and then moves on.

The Hare twitches again and turns in her sleep.

A languid sound of music drifts through the trees and rouses the Hare.

She stretches, loose-jointed and supple. Quivers, anticipating the new day.

She stares, golden-eyed, at the narrow path that cuts through the field.

Listens to the soft notes scrolling through the Old Man's Beard.

Pliny blows soft breath on the wildflowers.

White stars lead the way, and Hare starts her journey.

The Musician pauses, and, lowering his fiddle, watches as the shadows dance and metamorphose into creatures of antique tales. Elf and fairy, imp and nymph. Momentarily bewitched, he sees his own countenance mirrored in two golden orbs.

The charm breaks. He takes up his bow and plays.

"Fiddle-de-dee, fiddle-de-dee
The wasp will marry the bumble-bee.
Puss came dancing out of the barn
With a pair of bagpipes under her arm.
Pipe cat, dance bee
We'll have a wedding at half-past-three."

Enticed by the sweet sound, the Hare lopes off down the grassy path.

The music rises and is caught on the morning breeze. Swirling, falling, and then rising again, it joins the swallows that skim across the river's glassy surface, dipping their wings and beaks; igniting silver rings that spread and then float gently away.

The Hare watches the rowboats' steady rise and fall. She sees the long fingered grundylows playing with the turquoise fishes.

She waits, cautious, aware that the river has dangers. She sees the old ferryman counting Charon's pennies, whilst whistling softly to himself.

"Michael row the boat ashore, Hallelujah,
Michael row the boat ashore, Hallelujah,
Sister help to trim the sails, Hallelujah,
Sister help to trim the sails, Hallelujah,
Michael's boat is a musical boat, Hallelujah,
The trumpet sounds…"

Shades flicker along the riverbank.

Once again sweet music drifts on the gentle wind. Zephyr's serenade now muted, now clamorous. The Musician is crossing the timeworn bridge, his rhythm directed by the ghosts of Caesar's legions, marching to the orders of Mars.

Beneath the bridge, Melusine's handmaidens chant:

"Hurry, hurry, be on your way.
Don't linger long, for here the mermaids lurk."

And then they sink below the river's surface, their emerald scales glinting between water-smoothed pebbles of sienna, opal, cobalt grey and ivory black. The emerald green strands of waterweed disguise their tresses.

The Musician's shadow passes over them, and they are gone. He pauses and looks to where the Hare is waiting. He smiles and then continues on his way.

Several pairs of glittering jade eyes watch as the Hare crosses the bridge.

"There was an old woman,
And nothing she had,
And so this old woman,
Was said to be mad,
She'd nothing to eat,
She's nothing to wear,
She'd nothing to lose,
She'd nothing to fear,
She'd nothing to ask,
And nothing to give…"

The Hare catches up with the Musician just as he arrives in front of a low tumbledown cottage. The open door reveals a dark interior with shadowy outlines of a chair and a table, at which an old crone sits polishing an engraved copper urn. As she polishes, the etched figures dance and writhe. Her shrewd eyes rest on the Hare, and a spark of recognition momentarily lights up her face.

The crooked-backed woman smiles and wipes her hands on her apron. She chuckles and opens a book with yellowing pages and ink faded to sepia. She turns the page marked with the green and turquoise feather of a magpie's tail.

In the garden is a child's rusty swing, gently rocking. The chains and bolts, dried through misuse and neglect, squeal protest; astonished at the extravagance of the flowers and herbs that fill the borders, every hue, tint and tone vying for attention.

The Hare's golden eyes fix on the butterflies, the bees and the dragonflies, which flit and shimmer. Her ears are alert to the faint sound of children singing...

"See-saw Margery Daw
Jacky shall have a new master
He shall have but a penny a day
Because he can't work any faster."

Across the street, the Poet looks up from his book and listens. He watches the Musician and recognizes the tunes. Old tunes, telling tales from long ago.

"I remember well
The stories the old folk tell
Upon the hill which here is seen
Many a battle there have been
If it is true so I heard say
King George did here the dragon slay."

He looks back to the black, leather bound book. He turns the pages and studies the hieroglyphs, and is bewildered to see the red, gold and lapis twisting and turning, joining the music that still intrudes through the open window. He looks up and watches the old woman still seated at her table, their eyes meet and then he glances down, and for a moment is mesmerised by a pair of golden eyes.

In an oak panelled library the Sage ponders the ancient parchment that has just come into his posesssion. He is not familiar with the faint symbols and so turns to his bookshelves. He runs his bony fingers along the soft leather spines, quietly humming to himself along to the tune that drifts through the open door.

"Ring a ring a roses
A pocket full of posies
A-tishoo a-tishoo
We all fall down."

A distant roll of thunder wraps itself around the jaunty notes, muffling and subduing them.

Open book in his hands, the Sage returns to his desk under the fixed gaze of the wooden grotesques that furnish the room.

On the back of his chair sits an owl. It swivels its head to watch him, but then turns back to stare at the Hare, which is paused, quivering, watching, waiting on the threshold.

The Sage's gnarled fingers trace the ancient calligraphy.

"Magic, Sorcery, Witchcraft" he whispers.

The Owl swoops towards the motionless Hare.

Inside his workshop the Sculptor glances up.
A sudden shadow cast by silent wings. A hooked beak,
grasping talons, soot black eyes.

"To-wit-to-whoo."

An Old Woman with an owl perched on her crooked
shoulder, smiles secretly and walks away down the stony
path.

"In the moonlit field nearby,
I see an old witch-hare take fright.
But when she stops and to stare,
I whisper softly,
'Hey there, stay there',
But then she is gone, sheltered by the night."

The Sculptor turns back to his task. Strokes the smooth pale
wood and takes up his chisel. Another whorl of sweet
smelling oak spirals down. Slowly he perfects the likeness of
a fleeing hare, its swift, never-ending, relentless journey
captured forever.

"The owl is wary, the owl is wise.
He knows all the names of the stars in the skies,
He hoots and toots and lives by his wits,
But mostly he sits, and he sits."

Beneath the castle walls the old woman stops to rest.
Invisible in the soot dark shadow.

A peacock shrieks. A fox yelps. The rising moon casts soft
shadows through the topiaried yews, bringing to life
dragon wings, serpents' tails.

The Hare skips softly, wending her way through the maze
towards a light that shines brightly from a lattice window,
casting a pool of yellow light. Here she stays, listening,
watching, expectant.

Wizards peep and mutter from the castle ramparts.

High above, where the fog is curling and creeping sits the Writer. Above him carved oak-beams ornamented with leaves, flowers and berries, and a painted ceiling of lapis lazuli, sprinkled with gilded stars and pearly moons.

A large fireplace is guarded by stone sentinels; two mute swans with wings outstretched, and a large blind carp, its tail curled like a serpent.

Fitful lightning joins the flickering candlelight. It illuminates the tapestries that line the warm sandstone walls, animating the figures, causing birds to fly, the beasts to flee, and to interweave with the musing of the Writer.

The only sound is the scratching of his quill.

"All that we see or seem
Is but a dream within a dream."

The Writer pauses for a moment and stares thoughtfully at the tapestries.

A snow-white unicorn is transfixed by its own image reflected in the silver mirror held by his flaxen haired mistress. Blue and green-jewelled birds flit among vermillion and scarlet trees. The watchful Hare hears the hunters' horns in the distance.

The Writer picks up his pen again.

"Maids all in a ring and all the birds sing,
Knights and knaves a prancing."

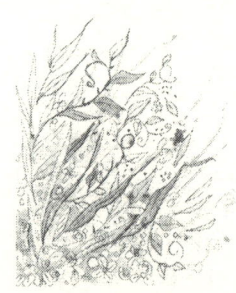

Below in the garden the Hare is alert. The storm clouds draw apart and unveil the moon that casts a silver light all around. The rustling of wet leaves and the tip-tap of raindrops mingle with the Musician's new refrain that drifts on the cooling air.

"Say it's only a paper moon
Sailing over a cardboard sea
But it wouldn't be make-believe
If you believed in me.

It's a Barnum and Bailey world
Just as phony as can be
But it wouldn't be make-believe
If you believed in me."

Deep in the woods, high on the hill, in a moonlit clearing beneath a blasted oak, sleeps the Hunter. His velvet black dogs dream with their heads on their paws.

A crooked-backed woman steps soundlessly from the shadows and peers with narrowed eyes at the hunter and his hounds, and then moves quickly away. As she fades back into the gloom, a short-lived breeze rustles the leaves around her.

The Hare breaks from the cover of the woods with leaps and bounds, and dashes off down the hill towards a narrow lane.

In the lane an old woman shuffles long, humming softly.

The lane twists and turns down to the river. A silver thread glimpsed through the rising morning mist.

Fleetingly, the Musician sees the bent silhouette, but it abruptly disappears into the shadowy obscurity of the overhanging trees. The Musician picks up his fiddle and continues his eternal journey. Tall willows reach down over him, but then a gentle wind parts the skirts of green and gold, and he passes through.

"Willow weep for me
Willow weep for me
Bend your branches to the ground and cover me
Listen to my plea
Hear me willow and weep for me..."

The Poet-Wanderer hears the distant melody and turns.
He watches as a glistening dewdrop, a shimmering crystal,
slides gently down the iridescent blue and turquoise back
of a bright eyed kingfisher.

The air is hushed.

Among the tangled roots, on a bed of moss, sleeps the Hare.
Beside her, six leverets quiver and tremble, dreaming on,
dreaming on.

"A sight to dream of, not to tell?"

"Am I just a dreamer of dreams?"

List of Quotations (First Lines)

To bring music and poetry to Hare's Journey, the author has woven in snippets of some well-loved nursery rhymes, poems and songs as listed below. All other verse is original.

Page 8 *"Fiddle-de-dee"* (traditional nursery rhyme).

Page 12 *"Michael Row the Boat Ashore"* (traditional spiritual song).

Page 16 *"There Was an Old Woman and Nothing She Had"* (traditional nursery rhyme).

Page 20 *"See-Saw Margery Daw"* (traditional nursery rhyme).

Page 22 *"I remember well"* (traditional verse).

Page 24 *"Ring a ring of roses"* (traditional nursery rhyme).

Page 30 *"The Owl is wary, the owl is wise"* (traditional verse).

Page 32 *"All that we see or dream"* from *"Dream within a Dream"* (poem by Edgar Allan Poe).

Page 36 *"Say it's Only a Paper Moon"* from *"It's Only a Paper Moon"* (popular song written by Harold Arlen and published in 1933, with lyrics by E. Y. Harburg and Billy Rose. Lyrics © Warner/Chappell Music, Inc., Universal Music Publishing Group, Shapiro Bernstein & Co. Inc., S.A. Music.)

Page 42 *"Willow Weep for Me"* (popular song by Ann Ronell, written in 1932. Lyrics © The Songwriters Guild Of America).

Page 44 *"A sight to dream of"* from *"Christabel"* (poem by Samuel Coleridge, 1772–1834).

Page 44 *"Am I just a dreamer of dreams?"* inspired by *"Ode"* (poem by Arthur O'Shaughnessy 1844-1881)

Sandra Bright studied at the Harrow School of Art. She is an art tutor in Berkshire, and a freelance illustrator and artist.

http://www.sandrabright.co.uk

Edited by Danielle Ward

Made in the USA
Charleston, SC
17 May 2015